D0042620

Text copyright © 1995 Hilary McKay
Illustration copyright © 1995 Tony Kenyon

First published in Great Britain in 1995
by Victor Gollancz

This edition published in 2009
by Hodder Children's Books

The right of Hilary McKay to be identified as the Author and Tony Kenyon
as the Illustrator of the Work has been asserted by them in accordance with
the Copyright, Designs and Patents Act 1988.

1

All rights reserved. Apart from any use permitted under UK copyright law,
this publication may only be reproduced, stored or transmitted, in any form,
or by any means with prior permission in writing from the publishers or in
the case of reprographic production in accordance with the terms of
licences issued by the Copyright Licensing Agency and may not be
otherwise circulated in any form of binding or cover other than that in
which it is published and without a similar condition being imposed on the
subsequent purchaser.

All characters in this publication are fictitious and any resemblance to real
persons, living or dead, is purely coincidental.

A Catalogue record for this book is available from the British Library

ISBN: 978 0 340 97027 0

Printed in the UK by CPI Bookmarque, Croydon, CR0 4TD

The paper and board used in this paperback by Hodder Children's Books
are natural recyclable products made from wood grown in sustainable
forests. The manufacturing processes conform to the environmental
regulations of the country of origin.

Hodder Children's Books is a division of Hachette Children's Books
338 Euston Road, London NW1 3BH
An Hachette UK Company
www.hachette.co.uk

The Magic
in the Mirror

Written by
HILARY McKAY

Hodder
Children's
Books

A division of Hachette Children's Books

Chapter One

Anna gazed at her reflection in the bowl of a spoon and was pleased to see that it was still upside down. Even when she turned the spoon over it was upside down.

Anna Lee lived with her parents in a flat in Paradise House. She was nine years old and she believed in magic, and for years and years she had assumed that everyone else did as well. This was because the only sensible explanation she could think of for her upside-down reflection was that somewhere between her face and the spoon a bit of magic got in the way.

One day she happened to mention this idea to Danny O'Brien and Nathan Amadi, who were also nine years old and lived in flats in Paradise House. Danny and Nathan said she was mad.

Instead of bothering to argue, Anna rushed off and borrowed two soup spoons from her mother (without asking) and handed one to each of the boys. They inspected their upside-down reflections with astonishment and disbelief.

"They must be from the joke shop," said Danny, who had recently spent every penny he possessed on a lifelike and disgusting trick snake that wriggled in at one ear and out at the other. "How much did they cost?"

"They're just ordinary spoons," said Anna.

"What would happen if we hammered them flat?" asked Nathan.

"They would break!" said Anna, hastily retrieving her mother's spoons. "Hammer your own spoons flat!"

"I'm sure it doesn't happen with all spoons," said Danny. "I'd have noticed if it did."

"Try it yourself, then," replied Anna, and Danny did and discovered he was wrong. It worked with every spoon that he and Nathan tried. Hammering them flat was much more difficult than Nathan had supposed (not least because no one would lend him a hammer), and eventually the boys were forced to agree that Anna was right. Spoon magic was true.

"Not that it's any use," remarked Nathan.

Anna pointed out that if spoon magic was true then other sorts of magic might equally well be possible.

"Ghosts and dragons and magic spells and flying carpets and genies in bottles," she added optimistically.

Nathan and Danny admitted that a flying carpet would be very useful, and one wet and boring afternoon they tried out every rug and mat and piece of carpet in Paradise House, including Old McDonald the caretaker's ancient and hairless doormat. Nothing, not even the two Miss Kent sisters' home-made hearthrug, showed the slightest sign of taking off. Danny and Nathan were not surprised and gave up the search for useful magic, but Anna did not. She continued to rub likely looking bottles in the hope of discovering a genie

and to gaze at her upside-down reflection in spoons. She found this one small piece of useless magic endlessly comforting. It meant anything could happen.

One day a new supply of books appeared in the school library. Amongst them was an encyclopaedia of science. Nathan, attracted by its hugeness and the vast number of illustrations it contained, chose it for his weekend reading book, carted it back to Paradise House and discovered the explanation for upside-down reflections in spoons.

"Bother!" said Nathan aloud and read the page again. There was no doubt about it; there it was, set out perfectly plainly in the section on mirrors, with plenty of pictures to make everything clear. Nathan (who lived on the ground floor) carried the book up two flights of stairs to Danny (who lived under the attic) and they both agreed it was

10

rather bad news.

"Don't let's tell Anna," said Danny, as Nathan started back down the stairs again, but Anna (who lived on the floor in between Danny and Nathan) popped out unexpectedly at that moment and asked, "Don't tell Anna what?"

This meant that Anna had to be told and she took the news extremely badly. Danny and Nathan thought it very unfair that rather than blaming whoever had written the encyclopaedia for such dismal information, she blamed them instead.

"It's not our fault," protested Nathan.

"Pigs!" said Anna.

"Just like a girl!" remarked Danny. This was always the quickest way of annoying Anna, as Danny knew perfectly well.

"Fancy crying," said Nathan.

"I'm not crying!" said Anna, sniffing and furious. "And you cried yourself last week when Danny hit you. I remember."

"I didn't hit him!" said Danny indignantly. "He
fell over when I tackled him and whacked my
elbow with his nose."

"And I didn't cry," added Nathan. "My eyes
watered. Anyone's would have."

Anna replied that she did not care, she hated
their book, they were useless, stupid boys and she
would never speak to them again. Then she
marched back into her flat, collected yet another
of her mother's few remaining spoons, and sat on
her bed staring miserably at her completely
understandable, scientifically explainable reflection
and thinking how boring everything was going to
be in a world where there was no magic left.

"I just knew we shouldn't have told her,"
remarked Danny when Anna had gone.

"She can't help being a soppy girl," said Nathan
kindly, and they agreed to forgive her. The next
morning when they met Mrs Lee on the stairs they

sent a message to Anna inviting her out to play
football, adding that it didn't matter about the
spoons.

"What about the spoons?" asked Anna's mother.

"They're not magic like she thought they were,"
explained Danny.

"Oh," said Anna's mother, who had noticed a
strange lack of spoons in her kitchen for some
time, and she went back home and had a proper
count and then knocked at Anna's bedroom door.

"Four soup spoons, most of the dessertspoons,
those two big serving spoons I bought only a week
or so ago, all the teaspoons, except the plastic
ones," she announced to Anna, "have vanished!
And Danny tries to tell me they're not magic!"

Anna sighed, slid off her bed and began a
gloomy spoon hunt. It took ages because her room
was spectacularly untidy, but in the end most of
them were unearthed. Her mother sat on the bed
and watched, tactfully trying not to notice the

state of the room. It was a joke between Anna and her mother that untidy bedrooms were a family tradition that Anna would grow out of in time.

"Danny and Nathan asked if you'd like to go out and play football."

"I'm fed up with Danny and Nathan," replied Anna. "I'm fed up with boring boys and boring football and boring science." And she stared sadly at her reflection in the last soup spoon before handing it over to her mother.

"I'd love to know why you wanted all these spoons," remarked her mother, "unless it's very private."

"I liked looking at the magic," explained Anna. "Only it isn't."

"What isn't?"

"My upside-down face."

"Oh!" exclaimed Anna's mother, after a moment's puzzled thought. "You've found out why your reflection is the wrong way up!"

"It was in Nathan's library book," said Anna, "and it's boring science, not magic."

"But why does it matter so much?" asked Anna's mother, because it was obvious that to Anna it mattered very much indeed.

"It proved there was magic," said Anna, so sadly that her mother suddenly understood. She tried to think back to the time when she had stopped believing in magic. Well, perhaps I didn't ever stop, she told herself when nothing came to mind, and instead she started trying to remember being nine years old. It was very difficult. Nine years old was all confused with being seven and eight and ten until she recalled that when she was nine she'd had terrible measles. No one had been allowed to come and play with her and she'd been bored and cross and lonely and her mother had—

"I learnt to juggle!" she said out loud.

"What?" asked Anna.

"I've just remembered," exclaimed her mother.

"Your great-grandmother's Chinese toy-box!" and she hurried out of the room.

"I didn't know I had a great-grandmother," said Anna, following.

"Of course you did; you had four," replied her mother, fetching a chair from the kitchen and carrying it into her bedroom.

"Four?" asked Anna.

"And eight great-great-grandmothers," said her mother, climbing on to the chair and rummaging about in the top of her wardrobe.

"Eight?"

"And sixteen great-great-great-grandmothers. I know it's up here somewhere."

"All Chinese?"

"Of course!" said her mother. "And thirty-two great-great-great-great-grandmothers. Here it is!" and she pulled out a small wooden box.

"There!" she said, and passed it down to Anna.

Chapter Two

It was very small for a toy-box. It was hardly
bigger than a large shoe box, and was made of
wood and painted red. On the lid was a beautiful
picture of a dancing dragon in green and gold.

"She painted that," said Anna's mother.

"Who did?"

"Your great-grandmother."

Anna opened the box and looked inside. She
saw three brightly coloured balls, two stiff wooden
dolls, and something else, folded underneath. The
balls were very worn and not at all the sort that
Anna usually played with. They were made of

coloured cloth, sewn up in segments like the slices of an orange.

"Juggling balls," said Anna's mother, picking them up. "Filled with sawdust."

Anna was looking at the dolls. They were carved out of wood and wore glued-on silk clothes. Their faces were empty painted faces, not smiling or sad or worn or interesting in any way. If their clothes had not been so faded they could have been brand new.

"They don't look very played with," Anna remarked.

"I think she must have been like you and not cared very much about dolls," replied her mother. "My mother didn't either, and nor did I. I used to play with the juggling balls, though. I learnt to juggle with them. I wonder if I can still do it."

Anna forgot about there being no more magic as she watched her mother throwing and catching the bright silk balls. They rose and fell in enchanting loops, faster and faster through the air.

"I'm glad I haven't forgotten," said her mother. "Haven't you found it yet?"

"What?" asked Anna, suddenly coming out of her dream.

"This!" said her mother. "The best thing of all!" and she lifted the bundle from the bottom of the box, shook out stiff folds of green and gold silk, and held up a little Chinese coat.

The sleeves and front were embroidered with

butterflies and birds, the hem was edged with a line of yellow daisies, and all across the back danced a gorgeous scarlet dragon.

The moment Anna saw the Chinese coat all the soreness and disappointment that she had felt since Nathan showed her his science encyclopaedia disappeared like smoke in the wind.

"I'm afraid it's had a hard life," remarked her mother, and Anna saw that one sleeve of the coat was badly torn, the stitches of the dragon were pulled and broken and the silk had a buckled, bumpy look like paper that has been soaked and dried.

"How did it get like that?" asked Anna.

"You may well ask!" replied her mother. "Aren't you going to put it on?"

When Anna tried the coat on they found that the Chinese toy-box had been remembered just in time. The coat was almost too small and only really comfortable after Anna swopped the thick

top she was wearing for her thinnest T-shirt.

"Don't you think it's very nearly magic," asked her mother, "to be wearing a coat your great-grandmother wore in China all those years ago?"

"Do you know what she looked like?" asked Anna.

"You'll see if you look in a mirror," replied Mrs Lee. "You look like me and I look like my mother and I remember that she told me she looked just like hers. I expect your great-grandmother looked very like you!"

Anna looked in the mirror and the face of her Chinese great-grandmother looked out at her.

"Perhaps she looked like her mother," she thought, "and her mother's mother, and her mother's mother's mother!" It was incredibly strange to think of all those long ago little girls with faces like her own.

"I wish they were here now," she said aloud.

"Who?" asked her mother.

"My Chinese great-grandmothers."

"Goodness knows what they'd think of the state of your room," replied her mother.

"Family tradition," said Anna.

"I know," agreed her mother, "but I honestly don't think that in a thousand years of Chinese grandmothers any of them lived in such a mess as you do!"

"Not in a thousand years?" asked Anna.

"At least," said her mother.

"Pity to tidy it up then," said Anna.

Nathan and Danny and Anna made friends again that same day. They played their own version of football, one-a-side and one (supposedly unbiased) in the shared goal, and Anna volunteered to be in goal to make up for her horribleness the night before. Whoever was in goal was also expected to referee and the game was always more exciting when Anna did this. The decisions came much faster and the score was much higher than usual. This time Anna allowed it to mount up to eight – all before she decided she had been noble enough for one day, and then she invited the boys to come and see her mother juggling.

"Crikey!" said Danny, when Anna's mother had obligingly juggled for them. "Can you juggle anything?"

"What sort of anything?" asked Anna's mother.

"Oranges?" suggested Danny, glancing round the room and catching sight of the fruit bowl.

"Certainly," said Anna's mother, and she juggled first with oranges and then (at Anna's suggestion) with bananas and then with a mixture of both.

"What about eggs?" asked Nathan hopefully.

Anna's mother caught the bananas and oranges and put them carefully back in the fruit bowl.

"Not eggs," she said firmly to Nathan.

All the same they were very impressed by her skills and when Danny revealed that his mother

could turn cartwheels and had once been persuaded to hang by her heels from the climbing frame in the park, Nathan suggested that they collect their mothers together one day and form a small circus.

"Why, what can yours do?" asked Danny.

Nathan replied that she couldn't do anything but added that he was sure she could be trained. That day ended very cheerfully; spoons were not mentioned and neither was the Chinese coat. In its own way the Chinese coat was as exciting and lovely a thing as spoon magic had ever been and Anna was determined to keep it like that. She hid it carefully out of sight when the boys were visiting, but all through the talk of circuses and juggling and whether Nathan's mother could be induced to leap through hoops the thought of it glowed in Anna's mind. It hung beside her bed when she went to sleep and was the first thing she saw when she woke in the morning.

*   *   *

It was very, very early and very, very silent. Except for Anna, Paradise House and all its occupants were bound in sleep. It made Anna, who felt unusually awake herself, remember the story of the palace full of people who had fallen asleep for a hundred years.

Very quietly Anna climbed out of bed, slipped on the Chinese coat and went to look at her great-grandmother's face in the mirror. It smiled back out at her, wide awake and twinkling. Anna held up her arms so that the green and gold butterfly sleeves slid down to her elbows and looked at their reflection and thought, There are her hands, and she waved to her great-grandmother and her great-grandmother waved back.

"I wish it was a bigger mirror," said Anna. Her feet, when she looked down, just looked like her ordinary bare feet. They did not look like they belonged to her great-grandmother.

"They don't match," she told her reflection, and

then she remembered that in the entrance hall of Paradise House there was an enormous old mirror, big enough to see her whole self in at once. Before she had thought twice about it she had tiptoed cautiously out of the flat and was sneaking carefully down the stairs.

The mirror in the hall was one of the few things in Paradise House left over from the old days. Although its heavy frame was cracked and the surface of the glass was always faintly misty, it was a kindly mirror. There was a goldness in its silvering that made even the oldest Miss Kent look smooth skinned and young again. It made Anna in her bare feet and Chinese coat look perfectly beautiful.

Gazing into the mirror Anna noticed at once how bright the colours of the coat were. All the stains and shabbiness of age were lost in the reflection. For the first time Anna saw that gold threads were woven into the scarlet of the dragon so that in the early morning sunlight he looked like a dragon painted in flame. She spun round and round and the Chinese coat left a trail of its own brightness in the air around it, like the trail of light that follows a sparkler in the dark.

"If I could jump far enough it would make a rainbow," thought Anna, pausing dizzily for a moment. Her reflection, which had carried on spinning for quite a long time after she had stopped, looked thoughtfully out at her.

"I need something high to take off from," continued Anna, gazing round the empty hall, and then she realized that the end of the stair banister was reflected in the mirror.

"Perfect!" said Anna, and her reflection in the mirror nodded in agreement.

Banister sliding was definitely not allowed at Paradise House. It was very high up on the long list of things forbidden by Old McDonald, among such crimes as the smuggling in of livestock

(Danny), the dismantling of the fuse box (Nathan) and the indoor use of roller skates, which had been Anna's particular offence. However it was still very early. Old McDonald was fast asleep and out of the way. As long as Anna was quiet there was no one to stop her doing exactly as she liked. Cautiously at first, and then faster and faster, she began banister sliding, watching in the mirror at the end of each ride for the lovely moment when her reflection would flash into view.

It did make a rainbow.

Chapter Three

That was the beginning of Anna's early morning visits to the mirror in the entrance hall.

From the first time that Anna had crept downstairs in her Chinese coat she had an odd feeling that she was not quite alone. Often she had thought that it would be enjoyable to have a Chinese friend to play with, and now in her mind her reflection became that person. It was nice to pretend that it really was her Chinese great-grandmother whose eyes sparkled with mischief in the big old mirror.

"She looks good fun," said Anna, who found it

slightly surprising that someone from so long ago could be anything but quiet and demure until she remembered the painted dragon on the toy-box lid and the family tradition of untidy bedrooms, and added understandingly, "Perhaps she didn't know that she was going to be a great-grandmother."

She certainly didn't look like a great-grandmother.

One morning Anna took the Chinese toy-box downstairs with her.

"I thought you might like to see them again," she remarked, unpacking the dolls and holding them up.

"I don't play with dolls," said the expression on the face in the mirror as plainly as if she had spoken.

"Neither do I," agreed Anna, "but I wish I could juggle. I've been trying and trying but I can't."

The face in the mirror shone with interest at the appearance of the juggling balls, and when Anna tried to do it while looking at her reflection instead of anxiously watching her hands she found that juggling became much easier. The hands of the girl in the glass seemed to know exactly how to move between the bright silk balls, and the balls themselves flew up and down as neatly and reliably as if they were on strings.

I wonder if everything is easier if you do it in a mirror, thought Anna and began to test the idea straight away.

At first it seemed as if it might be true. Cartwheels, that in the past had always been lopsided, wobbling affairs, turned into spinning circles of green and gold when performed in front of the mirror. The little boxes of folded paper that her mother had tried for years to teach her to make suddenly became possible when Anna concentrated on her reflection's nimble fingers instead of her own. Anna grew very hopeful and took her maths homework down, but was

disappointed to find that the answers did not immediately appear written in the mirror.

"Pity," said Anna. "That would have been a useful sort of magic."

Anna was almost allowing herself to believe in magic again. It was midsummer and she got into the way of slipping out of bed for half an hour at dawn and then returning to sleep solidly till breakfast time. Nothing was different; nothing unusual happened; but in those snatches of time, when Anna was the only person awake in the whole house, the air seemed thick with enchantment. It was not just the excitement of being out so secretly and early, or the extra reflected brightness of the Chinese coat, or the added cleverness of Anna when she was wearing it that made everything so entrancing. There was something else that she had begun to notice.

Just as when you stare at a bright light and the image stays with you after you glance away, floating in front of your eyes, so Anna discovered that if she looked for long enough at the reflection of the Chinese coat in the mirror there would come a time when out of the corner of her eye she would catch a glimpse of scarlet and green and gold. It was as if someone wearing a Chinese coat like her own had only that moment dashed out of sight. It was very odd, but no more frightening than a sudden gleam of sunlight, or a wave from a friend. Anna called it the "flash" and she found it gave her good ideas.

It was the flash that woke her in the mornings. She would open her eyes and find it disappearing out of the bedroom door. While she was earnestly juggling in front of the mirror she would glimpse it sliding down the banisters, encouraging her to slide as well, which she did very enthusiastically, shooting down over and over again in order to admire the rainbow effect of her reflection in the mirror. This occupation very nearly ended Anna's early morning adventures. The thump of her feet penetrated through to the basement and woke Old McDonald who slept underneath.

"Burglars!" thought Old McDonald, who had always longed for an opportunity to tackle burglars, and he heaved himself out of bed. Luckily for Anna, the flash of colour led her back to safety just as Old McDonald, armed with a frying pan and dressed in an ancient dufflecoat, wellington boots and an orange and yellow knitted teacosy, marched into the hall. He was still in his burglar-tackling kit searching for clues when people began to be up and about.

"Did you find anything?" asked Anna's mother, when she heard his story.

"I found these," said Old McDonald and produced three silk-covered balls from his pocket.

"Oh!" exclaimed Anna's mother. "Those belong to Anna! You should be more careful, Anna; it would be a shame to lose them after we have kept

them safe all these years."

"Sorry," said Anna, going red as she took the balls from Old McDonald. "I must have dropped them."

"No harm done," replied Old McDonald.

"I'm glad you didn't find any burglars," said Anna's mother. "Not that I can imagine why burglars would come here! It's not as if there is anything to steal!"

"Something woke me up," said Old McDonald stubbornly, "and if it wasn't burglars, what was it?"

"Old houses like this do make strange noises," remarked Anna's mother. "I used to lie awake imagining all sorts when we first moved in. I suppose I've got used to it now."

"I've been living here for sixty years on and off and I never heard anything like that since the war," replied Old McDonald, looking rather hard at the crimson-faced Anna. "Only once since the air raids and that was this one that time too. Roller skates!

Five o'clock on Christmas morning! I've not forgot!"

"You nearly got me into trouble," Anna told her reflection severely. It did not look sorry.

"We will have to be more careful," she continued, but the face that smiled back at her from the mirror was not at all the face of someone who bothered too much about being careful, and, as if to prove this, the very next morning the flash disappeared straight out of the front door before Anna was hardly down the stairs.

At first Anna was astonished and then she was excited. It had never occurred to her that she could go outside and even as she struggled with the bolts and locks of the front door she had doubts about whether she really should. She could not help thinking that her sleeping parents would probably not approve. Also it seemed a pity to have to leave behind her beautiful reflection.

"But I can always come back in," she told herself, and then found that she didn't need to because her reflection was already outside and waiting for her. She saw it at once, bobbing up and down in Old McDonald's basement windows.

Except for a large rose bed belonging to Old McDonald, the garden of Paradise House consisted mostly of washing lines and rather worn-out grass, but even so, shining with dew on a midsummer morning, it looked quite beautiful. There were a few roses out on the rose bushes and Anna was admiring and sniffing them when, out of the corner of her eye, she caught sight of the green and gold flash of colour disappearing round the side of the house. It obviously had no interest in roses or dew-soaked grass. It led Anna straight to the dustbins.

Old McDonald was in charge of the dustbins. There was an extra special "luxury" one that he kept separately for himself and seven ordinary

ones, all in a tidy row, for everyone else. "Messing about with them bins" was another thing on Old McDonald's list of criminal offences. He would really have preferred the people of Paradise House to think of some other way of disposing of their rubbish so that he could always keep the dustbins neat and clean and empty, and he protected them as carefully as if they were seven gold mines.

Anna saw at once why the flash had led her to them. There was a cat sitting on the middle bin. It was large and bony and had dirty white fur and was obviously deep in furious thought. Old McDonald's latest dustbin protection scheme was to balance a large lump of concrete in the middle of each lid and Anna saw that the cat was staring at these obstacles with a disgusted expression on its face.

"It's all right," said Anna, who understood the situation at once. "I'm here now!"

It took no time at all to shove Old McDonald's

dustbin protectors on to the ground, and then they found what the cat was hoping for almost immediately. Half a cheese sandwich, Chloe's yesterday's breakfast's scrambled egg and a tin of tuna fish that had looked very strangely green to Nathan's mother; all disappeared in a matter of moments. Anna replaced six of the dustbin lids, stroked the cat who had curled up on a pile of old newspapers in the seventh bin, wiped her hands on the wet grass, dried them on her Chinese coat and went to bed feeling very pleased with herself.

"Something's been at them bins," grumbled Old McDonald later that day, "and if I get hold of it I shall give it What For!"

"Perhaps it was a cat," suggested Anna's mother innocently, "although how a cat could shift those dreadful huge lumps of concrete . . ."

Anna's mother broke off, catching sight of an awful expression of extreme goodness that was spreading over Anna's face.

"Perhaps it was an enormous cat," said Danny hopefully. "Escaped from the zoo. A tiger or a lion or a leopard or a puma."

"Pumas are wild in Devon," put in Nathan. "I saw a programme about them on TV."

"I wish I lived in Devon then," said Danny.

Anna's mother glanced at Anna again, and saw to her great relief that Anna's face was returning to its normal self.

"Those lumps of concrete," she continued. "I very nearly dropped one on my foot last night—"

"You picked it up wrong then," interrupted Old McDonald.

"I'm sure someone will hurt themselves. They must be far too heavy for the poor old Miss Kents."

"They don't have that much rubbish," said Old McDonald heartlessly.

"Really!" exclaimed Anna's mother when he had

gone. "Awkward old man! I notice his own bin doesn't have a great big boulder. It serves him right if people don't put back his horrible stones. The poor Miss Kents!"

"It would be jolly exciting if a puma crept up on one of the old Miss Kents while she was heaving away at one of those lumps of concrete," remarked Nathan cheerfully.

"It would be terrible," contradicted Danny at once. "They would probably shoot the puma!"

"You boys are worse than Old McDonald!" complained Anna's mother.

"And what are you looking so innocent about, Anna?"

"I didn't know I was," replied Anna.

"That's twice!" she told her reflection the next morning. "Twice already!" And then, because it was another lovely sunny morning, she went outside to look for the cat.

Chapter Four

The cat (who was sulking on the dustbin lids again) jumped up when Anna arrived.

"Which bin then?" asked Anna. "I'm not opening them all!"

The cat, after a moment's thought, indicated the bin of its choice. Anna heaved aside the lump of concrete, and after a short search they discovered half a packet of defrosted fish fingers and a Cornish pasty with one bite taken out of it.

"Danny's gran made that," Anna told the cat. "Listen!" and she rapped it gently with her knuckle.

"Danny's gran's cooking always sounds like that," explained Anna.

The cat ate the fish fingers, spat scornfully at the pasty and wandered away. Anna replaced the dustbin lid and the concrete block and began a wild game of tag with her reflection in the basement windows which ended, quite suddenly, in bed.

"Mind the pond!" she said sleepily, and woke up from a dream of a paved garden, a square patch of lily-covered water, and a little girl laughing and dripping in a Chinese coat.

"That's how it got soaked," said Anna.

"Hurry up, Anna!" said her mother. She was standing over the bed, unwinding Anna from the tangle of her quilt. "It's after eight; you'll be late for school. And you shouldn't go to bed in that Chinese coat and LOOK AT THE STATE OF YOUR FEET!"

Anna looked at her feet but could think of

nothing to say. They looked exactly as feet might be expected to look when their owner had played barefoot tag on a soaking lawn at five o'clock in the morning.

"I bet Danny and Nathan don't go to bed with feet in that state!" scolded Mrs Lee, as she hurried her in the direction of the bathroom and began to strip the bed. "ANNA!"

"What?" asked Anna, stopping on her way out of the door.

"WHAT'S THIS UNDER YOUR PILLOW?"

Anna stared in horror at her mother's latest discovery but she answered bravely, "It's a pasty Danny's gran made."

"A pasty?" asked her mother, taken aback.

"Yes," said Anna, as casually as she could, "Danny's gran made it for Danny's tea last night and Danny brought it out to show Nathan and me because Nathan was going to try to eat it—"

"Why was Nathan going to try to eat it?"

interrupted Anna's mother, and she picked up the pasty and stared at it in concern.

"Because Danny dared him," said Anna.

"Oh."

"But Nathan couldn't. Only one bite. So they put it in the bin, but I got it out again."

"And put it under your pillow?"

"Yes."

"But why?" persisted her mother. "If you were hungry—"

"Because it sounds like a box."

"Like a box?"

"When you bang it."

"One of us is going mad," said her mother. "I expect it's me. Go and get ready for school."

"Three times!" Anna told her reflection the next time they met. She was practising her juggling again, rather conceitedly because she was getting so good at it. She had progressed on to oranges and bananas with no difficulty at all.

"Two suns and a moon," said Anna dreamily, watching as the orange and yellow rose and fell, and rose and fell, and into her mind came the echo of Nathan's voice saying, "What about eggs?"

"Not eggs," said Anna out loud, and she stopped juggling and met the eyes of the girl in the mirror.

"Why not eggs?" asked those round brown eyes and her face had the look of innocence that Anna's parents always found so alarming.

"Eggs," said Anna to her reflection a few minutes later, "are easy!"

The face in the mirror sparkled with mischief.

"It's just a matter of catching them," said Anna smugly. "Same as anything else."

"I could do it forever," boasted Anna, and then blinked. Green and gold and scarlet light was dancing before her eyes.

* * *

The cat was very useful that morning.

"Lucky you were hungry," said Anna as it finished the third egg.

"Mum," said Anna later that day, "I broke three eggs."

"Three?" asked her mother.

"Sorry," said Anna.

"How?"

"Juggling," said Anna. "Why are you laughing?"

Old McDonald lost the dustbin war. The occupants of Paradise House (who usually obeyed his slightest whim) united in rebellion against the concrete blocks.

"Folk these days are soft!" grumbled Old McDonald, but he was forced to give in.

"The cat will be pleased," thought Anna when she heard the news, but the next morning the cat did not seem pleased at all. It seemed to have lost interest in being a dustbin cat and it mewed at the door of Paradise House until Anna was forced to let it in before it woke somebody up.

"I haven't got any eggs," she told it crossly, "and, anyway, you can't possibly be hungry. There were two whole sausages in the dustbin for your breakfast. I put them there myself."

The cat shrugged its shoulders and strolled across the hall to inspect itself in the mirror.

"You don't really look like that," Anna told it as it settled down to admire its sleek and beautiful reflection. "In real life you need a bath."

The cat took no notice. It appeared to be

watching something that was reflected over its shoulder, and when Anna turned to look at whatever it was she saw a gleam of green and gold and scarlet fading from a small door in the corner of the hall.

"That's Old McDonald's scullery," she said. "We can't go in there. We're not allowed. He keeps it locked."

The cat, who was not fond of Old McDonald, sniffed and made no comment. Plainly it thought Anna was just making excuses.

"Look!" said Anna impatiently, and she crossed the hall and tried the door just to show that she was right – and it was not locked.

The scullery was a cold, bare room filled with all the messiest things that belong to caretakers. Anna had only glimpsed its contents before. Piles of mops. Pots full of soaking paint brushes, shelves of bottles and polishes and mousetraps and empty jam jars. There was an old white sink with a

wooden draining board, a paint-splattered floor and a pile of paint tins stacked up in one corner.

Anna had always been fascinated by paint tins. She loved the excitement of prising away the lid, the jerk as it suddenly came free and the thrill of the sleek cool colours waiting inside, so different from the thin murky paints at school. One by one she opened all of Old McDonald's paint tins and when she came to a tempting pale-blue emulsion she could resist no longer and she dipped a handy paint brush into the surface of the paint.

It was very splashy paint. In no time at all there was an accidental line of blue drips running across the scullery floor and Anna had a moment of panic until she saw in large letters on the side of the tin

RINSES OUT EASILY WITH COLD WATER

"That's all right then," said Anna, and joined up the drips to make a dragon.

After a while Anna forgot about everything. There was an ice-blue dragon growing slowly and

perfectly on the red-tiled floor and nothing else in the world seemed to matter. It was quite a shock when the cat walked in.

It walked straight across the dragon (which was in no state to be trodden on, the paint being the sort that took twenty-four hours to dry) and left a trail of blue footprints on the scullery floor.

"Hey!" exclaimed Anna, and grabbed and missed. The cat slid through her hand and back across the dragon and headed out to the hall. It did not quite run, but it moved just fast enough to keep out of Anna's reach, and everywhere it went a pattern like large blue forget-me-nots followed after.

A completely soundless chase began: the cat with Anna always a little too far behind and the footprints always following. It was dreadful, and at the same time it was funny. Anna kept catching sight of her scurrying reflection almost helpless with silent giggles because there was something

uncanny about the way that every time the footprints became so pale as to be almost invisible the cat ran into the scullery for a fresh supply of paint. It was ages before Anna thought to rush in afterwards and shut the door.

"You stupid, stupid cat!" said Anna, and the cat rolled apologetically at her feet. It rolled right across the dragon and came up blue. Anna stared at it in speechless horror.

Until then the cat had only been mildly interested in the effects of the blue paint. Now it looked quite shocked and tried to get it off.

"Don't lick it!" exclaimed Anna. She had a horrible vision of trying to shave the cat and then she thankfully remembered the promise on the side of the tin.

"Lucky for you it comes off," she told the cat. "I shall just have to give you a bath, that's all."

The cat looked at Anna in disbelief.

"A bath," she repeated more confidently, and

she could not help thinking that it would be quite good fun to bath a cat.

The cat shook its head as if it was dreaming. Anna took no notice and filled the sink with water, testing the temperature carefully with her elbow as she had seen Chloe's mother test Chloe's bathwater. She made it very deep because something told her that once the cat was in the bath things would happen very quickly.

Anna picked up her troublesome companion and dumped it firmly in the sink and almost immediately the water became blue and the cat became white. Anna sighed with relief but the cat was not grateful. For two seconds it stood in the water, too astonished to move, and then, all at once, a huge blue tidal wave swept on to the floor and the cat leapt straight up into the air, out of Anna's hand, and went mad. It ran three times round the scullery without touching the floor and it knocked down every single thing it passed. It

passed a lot of things.

Anna wriggled out of her Chinese coat and on the cat's third circuit of destruction she managed to fling it over its head and then she seized the soggy, clawing, dripping bundle in both arms and ran with it out of the scullery.

Paradise House woke up that morning to crashes and shrieks and thumps and squeals coming from somewhere in the hall. One after another the frightened occupants collected on the stairs. Old McDonald arrived with his frying pan, and Nathan's father had just decided to ring the police, when Anna's mother suddenly appeared shrieking, "Anna! Anna! She's disappeared!"

"She'll be down with the boys," said Anna's father.

"She's not," said Nathan and Danny, and at that moment the scullery door was flung open and Anna appeared. She tore across the hall with her

struggling burden, just managing to hang on until she reached the front steps and then she thankfully let go. The cat disentangled itself and vanished round the corner, and Anna sat down on the steps. It was quite a long time before it occurred to her that she was not alone.

She glanced quickly over her shoulder and there they were. Laughing. Laughing and waiting for her to speak; and there she was, exhausted and suddenly miserable, with her private early morning world of magic in ruins around her.

"I don't know what's so funny," said Anna, and burst into tears.

Chapter Five

The list of things that Anna was banned from doing went on for so long that eventually she protested, "I'll never remember all that!"

"I'll write it out for you then," replied her father grimly, and he wrote:

YOU MUST NOT SNEAK OUT OF BED EARLY IN THE MORNING.

"I didn't sneak," objected Anna. "I just went."

YOU MUST NOT PLAY OUTSIDE ON YOUR OWN WITHOUT TELLING US WHERE YOU ARE.

"I wasn't on my own," murmured Anna.

"What did you say?" asked her father.

"Nothing," said Anna.

AND DON'T SLIDE DOWN THE
BANISTERS. WHAT IF YOU FELL?

"Why should I fall?" asked Anna scornfully.

DON'T PLAY AROUND THE DUSTBINS.

"I wasn't playing; I was helping the cat."

AND NEVER MEDDLE WITH THINGS
BELONGING TO OLD McDONALD AGAIN.

"Old McDonald didn't mind," said Anna.

This was astonishing but true. It had taken Old
McDonald two whole days to set everything to
rights: one to clean the paint from the hall, and
another to put the scullery back together, and yet
he did not mind. He thought it was a huge joke
and he never grew tired of calling, "Now then,
young Anna! Painted any stray cats lately?"

Anna got so tired of the question that she took
to avoiding Old McDonald, scurrying up the steps
to the front door and across the entrance hall to
the stairs before he could appear.

"Fancy Old McDonald being so nice," remarked
Danny, one day.

"Old McDonald is nice," said Nathan.

"I'd rather he was cross," replied Anna
ungratefully.

Anna's parents had been very cross. They

forced Anna to describe her secret dawn adventures in great detail, and the more they heard the crosser they became. When Anna attempted to explain that it was at least half the fault of her Chinese great-grandmother they said, "Really, Anna!" and became crosser still.

Her official punishment was to tidy her bedroom.

"Which should keep you out of mischief for months!" remarked her father. Not that there was any mischief to get into because they took away her Chinese coat. Anna's mother said it had aged more in three weeks in Anna's possession than it had done in three generations of Chinese ancestors.

"It wasn't meant for wearing in a sopping wet garden," said her mother severely. "Or as a painting overall, or for sliding down banisters, or for juggling with eggs in, or for wrapping up cats!"

The Chinese coat was sent to a very expensive

cleaners that dealt with such things. It was away for nearly a month and it felt like a year to Anna. With no Chinese great-grandmother to play with, and no green and gold flash of excitement to chase after, Anna felt lost. And had it been magic?

"I'm sure it was magic," she told herself over and over again, but as the weeks went by she grew less and less certain.

"I suppose I'll know when my coat comes back," she thought, although exactly how she would know she could not tell.

"And what if it isn't?" she wondered fearfully. Losing spoon magic had been bad enough. Losing Chinese coat enchantment would be much worse.

Then something unbelievable happened. The Chinese coat came home, more or less recovered from the effect of Anna's ownership, and Anna's mother wouldn't give it to her.

"It's going back in the toy-box," she told Anna, "with the juggling balls and dolls."

Anna raged and it did not work. Then she cried. Then she sulked. Then she begged. Then she went to bed and snuffled and her father came home and said, "Whatever is all the fuss about?" and took the Chinese coat out of the toy-box and hung it on Anna's bedroom door.

"Looking at it won't hurt," he remarked.

Anna fell asleep looking at it and woke up looking at it and it was early, early morning, just as it had always been.

"One more time," said Anna, and sneaked out of bed.

The Chinese coat felt very uncomfortable.

"It's shrunk," thought Anna, "or I've grown."

It pulled at the scruff of Anna's neck as she made her way downstairs. No bright flash of colour appeared to encourage her in her appalling behaviour and when she tiptoed round the corner to look at her reflection, it seemed that her Chinese great-grandmother glared back at her

most unconspiratorily. Her eyes said as clearly as possible, "Go back to bed!"

"Why should I?" asked Anna, forgetting how much she had longed to see her again and glaring back. "You got me into terrible trouble and now you've suddenly turned good! I shall do what I like! I'll go outside!"

Waves of disapproval followed Anna across the hall. She could feel them washing against her back. They infuriated her.

"I'm going into the garden," she said, and opened the door.

The garden that in the past had seemed so tempting now appeared most unmagic. It could not have looked plainer if it had been deliberately unenchanted.

"I shall go to the park then!" said Anna triumphantly, and marched back across the hall to see how her reflection was taking this bit of bad news.

There was no reflection. Anna stared at the place where it should have been and it was not until she had looked and looked that she realized there was no reflection because there was no mirror. The more she stared, the more muddled and tired and alarmed she became. And then she saw the tail end of a gleam of colour disappearing up the stairs. And she followed after and took off her Chinese coat and went to bed.

"That old mirror?" asked Old McDonald later that day. "It's been gone for weeks! I've took it down to see if I can do anything with the frame. Shame to let it go to pieces. I only noticed it on account of having to clean the hall after you and that cat played Old Scratch all around the houses! Painted any stray cats lately?"

"Not lately," said Anna, beaming up at him.

That same day the Chinese toy-box was carefully

repacked by Anna and her mother.

"For the next time," said Anna's mother, smiling at her.

"What next time?" asked Anna.

"There's always a next time," said her mother, but Anna had stopped listening and was admiring again the dragon painted on the lid.

"I can paint dragons," she thought, and she began to smooth out and fold the Chinese coat.

"There is magic," she whispered as she laid it in the box.

On top of the Chinese coat she put the three juggling balls.

"I can juggle with anything now," she said proudly.

"Except eggs!" said her mother. "What about the poor old dolls? I don't expect you ever looked at them!"

"Well, I don't play with dolls," said Anna, and put them in and closed the lid, and even as it

closed the memory of the flash of coloured
brightness and the face of her Chinese great-
grandmother sparkling from the mirror, faded and
was gone.

Still, there were three things left. She could
paint dragons. And juggle with anything,

including eggs (when hardboiled). And she knew, without doubt, that there was magic. That was the best thing of all.

Other books by Hilary McKay:

PUDDING BAG SCHOOL
The Birthday Wish
Cold Enough for Snow
A Strong Smell of Magic

Saffy's Angel
(Winner of the Whitbread Children's Book Award)
Indigo's Star
Permanent Rose
Caddy Ever After
Forever Rose

The Exiles
(Winner of the Guardian Children's Fiction Award)
The Exiles at Home
The Exiles in Love

Happy and Glorious
Practically Perfect

If you enjoyed The Magic in the Mirror, you might also like the other 'Paradise House' stories. Danny, Nathan and Anna continue their adventures in:

The Zoo in the Attic
The Treasure in the Garden
The Echo in the Chimney
The Surprise Party
Keeping Cotton Tail

The Surprise Party

Chapter One

Four children lived at Paradise House. There was Nathan Amadi, and his baby sister Chloe, Anna Lee, and Danny O'Brien. Nathan, Anna and Danny were all nine years old. It was Danny who discovered the tent.

Paradise House was an old London house divided into flats. There was a big scruffy garden, which everyone shared. The tent was in the garden. It was hanging from the washing line on the first hot day of the year.

At first Danny did not even know it was a tent. It was cream-coloured canvas, faded in places. It hung as if it was very heavy. It looked enormous and complicated and somehow exciting.

Danny went closer. It had a lovely smell, grassy and canvassy and a little bit musty. He ducked under a layer of canvas so that it hung all round him and shut his eyes and breathed in very deeply. It's a tent, thought Danny. This is what it smells like in a tent.

At that moment he was grabbed. The canvas was yanked away from his head, and there stood

the Old Miss Kent. There were two Miss Kents at Paradise House, Old Miss Kent and Young Miss Kent. The Old Miss Kent seemed hardly ever to go out, but she was here now.

"Oh, it's you, Danny," she said, trying very hard not to sound annoyed.

"I was just looking," said Danny.

The Old Miss Kent stroked and smoothed the canvas as if anxious to make sure that it had not been hurt.

"It's a tent, isn't it?" asked Danny.

"Of course it is."

"Is it yours?"

"Yes," said the Old Miss Kent, making an effort to be friendly. "I am airing it. I air it every year."

Then Danny got himself into trouble. It would never have happened to Nathan. Nathan was clever. He would have known before he asked just how such a question would sound. It wouldn't have happened to Anna either, because Anna understood how people felt. Danny was not like that, he understood animals better than people, and he never thought before he spoke.

"Are you going camping?" asked Danny.

It sounded very cheeky but it was not meant to do. After all, Danny did not know that the Old Miss Kent had not been camping for nearly fifty years. He did not know how old she felt, or that she took care of her tent, not because she was going camping, but because she remembered going camping, a long time ago.

"Are you going camping?" he asked again, when she did not reply.

Then the Old Miss Kent's cheeks went red, high up under her eyes, and her hands shook on the canvas and she said, "You are very rude. Very rude. Very rude indeed."

Danny was utterly astonished. Also ashamed, though he did not quite know why. After that he was always extra-polite to the Old Miss Kent, and she was extra-polite to him. Danny never told anyone about her tent. After a while he managed to put the memory way, way back to the part of his mind where he kept all the thoughts he would rather not think about.

The summer term at school came and went and the school holidays began. Old McDonald, the caretaker of Paradise House, began his enormous preparations for going to the seaside, and then he went to the seaside. Danny, Nathan and Anna did not.

"Next summer we will," their parents promised, but that was a whole year away, too far ahead to think about.

"You will have to make the best of London," said their parents, and took them out to parks and museums and the swimming pool as often as they could.

At first the best of London seemed not too bad

at all. Then, three weeks into the holiday, it suddenly got very bad indeed.

It was the sort of weather when it was hard not to quarrel. The air was thick and sticky with heat and the fumes from a million cars. It was the middle of August and the middle of a heatwave. Outside the school that the Paradise House children went to a large dusty notice sagged against the wall.

Holiday Club Here
8am to 6pm Every Day
Places Available!

Danny, Nathan and Anna, plodding home from the corner shop with lollies that melted faster than they could be eaten, looked quickly away.

"Bother my mum's new job!" said Anna as she tried to lick a trail of red juice that was running up to her elbow.

HOLIDAY CLUB
HERE
8am to 6pm Everyday
Places Available!

"Yes," agreed Danny, "and bother my gran! Fancy getting married at her age!" He took a large suck of lolly and the whole thing came off in his mouth and choked him.

"Bother my grandad too," said Nathan, gloomily gnawing off the wrong end of his ice-cream cone. "Fancy climbing ladders at his age!"

"Watch out!" said Anna suddenly, but it was too late. An avalanche of ice cream fell out of the bottom of Nathan's cone and landed on his trainer.

"Bother them all!" said Nathan, kicking savagely as it seeped into his laces.

The start of the trouble was Danny's gran who thoughtlessly arranged to have her honeymoon in the school summer holidays so that there was no one to look after Danny while his mother was at work. At first this did not matter at all. Anna's family lived in the flat below Danny and his mother, and Anna's mother offered to have Danny straight away.

95

"Thank you! Thank you!" said Danny's mum gratefully. "Anything to save him from You Know Where!"

You Know Where was the holiday club.

The second unexpected happening came two weeks later. Anna's mother heard she had got the job in the local library that she had applied for weeks before.

"Starting Monday!" she exclaimed, half-delighted and half-horrified, but even before she had begun to worry what to do about Danny and Anna, Mrs Amadi, Nathan's mother, had offered to have them both.

"Nathan would never forgive me if I let them go to That Place!" she said.

That Place was the holiday club too.